Show & Tell

By
Earvin P Eugene

Copyright © 2020 by Hearsay Online Co

Table Of Contents

Story Volume I
By
Earvin Phillip Eugene

Chapter 1: Health Problems

Since my early childhood, through adolescence and early adulthood, I have always been afflicted with some form of health issues and have had to rely on some medications for relief. Persistent and extreme breathing difficulties due to enlarged adenoids were misdiagnosed for asthma and allergies throughout my childhood and early adolescent years. This mis-diagnosis has exposed me to many years of taking unnecessary steroids and other anti-inflammatory medications with long term side effects. Later on, when the proper diagnosis was established and my enlarged adenoids were removed, I started breathing better. My experience and frustration, not only with the misdiagnosis but also with the long-term side effects of taking unnecessary medications have put me on a quest to learn everything I can about medications, understand their pathways, how they interact with the human body.

I had to adapt to my situation at a young age. I lived a sheltered life reading books, playing video games, and spending time with my siblings. My parents were hardworking middle class people, relying on grandparents and extended family to care for me when they were busy. I remember my parents helping with schoolwork when possible. Studies were paramount especially with a Catholic school curriculum. It was too difficult to focus with weight gain, difficulty breathing and sleeping with the cards I was dealt. I was naively optimistic and unaware of the gravity of my problems as I was accustomed to my issues. Playful at heart, I sought comfort from TV and had entertainment from my older brother and younger sister who were more active. Faith by mother presented hope for my condition and care as she is a nurse. My late great-aunt supported me through daily activities in most cases. Today, many family members remind me of the closeness I had to my great-aunt. One defining moment I had was when my childhood hero, my father showed a sense of nurture. My dad, usually a serious man focused on discipline and ambition stayed up all night ensuring I could sleep at night when I had an episode. He would hold me and position me to have access in my airways to breathe in order to sleep throughout the night. This was the beginning of a loss of innocence for me and a realization of my circumstance. I will never forget the moment my dad showed compassion to me. The providing strong figure in my life turned human.

Chapter 2: High School

The dawn of a new era, in the late 2000's the world seemed bright and hopeful. Energetic with youth, fit from exercise, and movement to suburban Setauket, Long Island from the urban westward Elmont. A valuable chapter of my life for mixing business with pleasure. I studied in honor and AP classes at Ward Melville High School and began a promising social life. I would play basketball with friends. Host house parties with classmates. We met together across town at parks, Smithaven mall, AMC movie theater, and each other homes. We laughed and shared provocative thoughts. We worked hard at our first jobs but had little worries when the weekend arrived. I started working at the mall at the U.S. Polo store. I had my first set of responsibilities opening up the store, organizing the store, and help made sales. I would help my family by providing nice discounted clothes. My friends and sister would visit for moral support. Times went by fast with a sense of community and spending time with co-workers.

Chapter 3: College Years

I attended Stony Brook University for better or worse I stayed home for college. I have a tightly knit family and I was advised being in a college town with plenty of resources that this was the best place to embark on my next journey. I was to study Pharmacology to understand medicine to deal with remitting ailments.

I spent my time in lecture halls, labs, Frat parties, and home. My experience was an introduction to maturity. I spent countless evenings watching lecture recordings, became a teaching assistant in organic chemistry, and performed research for the respected Harvard Lyman in cell biology. I was focused and my health was stable.

During my stint as a student I entered a serious relationship with my girlfriend. With my family support she lived at my house and we both attended Stony Brook University. This was different from past relationships and short-lived romances I had experienced. To have a comfort of a partner within your presence at most times. We would reach school, eat meals and sleep together. I had a taste of true commitment. Being in our youth still we experimented in many aspects of life. Attending "Brookfest", traveling to Boston, Myrtle Beach, and sharing life experiences with friends. I don't drink too much, I know the Budweiser became a mentality. Those days were wanderlust and only sustainable by youth. Troubling issues arrived with my serious relationship. No longer was there endearment and affection but malice. This had a toll on me. Nothing lasts forever.

Chapter 4: These Days

I found a passion for developing projects. I produced an app, PhotoGalah. An all in one app that had photo-sharing, simplified search engine, and video streaming. It was free and I advertised it on Facebook, LinkedIn, and Twitter. With increased presence and influence I was connected to

Lin Miao. Business was a new venture for me and I saw the success my family had so I wanted to try my luck. Lin Miao represented "Be Great Partners". He emulated lavish wealth and success. Lin hosted gatherings at his undisclosed mansion and many investors would converse. I was invited to Los Angeles, California. The city of angels!

With limited finances I took my chances from New York to Los Angeles as many have done before me. It was my opportunity to make a name for myself out west. At the summer soiree there was an open bar, aspiring entrepreneurs, executives and Lin. The mansion was on the hills overlooking the valley at night. After a few excursions at the party, I pursued Mr. Miao pitching my application idea. It was set in stone, we would work together. He offered me to stay at his place with few selected guests. I had some success, but to certain circumstances with the law our time was short-lived. I stayed optimistic took in the sights of Hollywood and returned home to New York.

The next best possibility to put my foot through the door was the Web Summit in Dublin, Ireland. This time I had the support of my father. This was a new battleground over the Atlantic Ocean. I was a small fish in a big pond. We stayed in a breakfast & inn at the heart of the city During the day I would attend conferences and meetings pitching my ideas. Receiving business cards and rubbing shoulders with the most influential of the tech industry. I was able to sell my app but for a small fortune. It seemed too expensive to run ads, produce growth, and expand markets. My father and I bonded over time well spent in a new country but I had fallen short. We took in the sights and tours of castles, farms, and European city life to past time for our return home.

Graduation had approached. Cap and gown ready, this was true success to my family. Short celebration and straight to work. I had to show signs of a real worker. Clock in the morning and clock out at night. I used my new degree as Pharmacologist and worked for Amneal Pharmacueticals as a scientist. My family was proud.

Chapter 5: Changes

With the remission of certain health problems. It was difficult to continue working. My family and friends became more concerned about me. I was in and out of the hospital and focused on staying home. These were troubling times, but I wanted more for myself.

I decided to go to medical school in St. Lucia to reconnect with my brother. I believed in a change of scenery and opportunity would be the perfect fit. My brother as a guide I hoped to be successful. We bonded about being two healthcare students abroad. Also, I built a relationship with housemates. We toured the island, enjoyed the environment when we could, and studied hard. There was a lot to see and experience. Sadly, I wasn't able to finish the program and had to take a leave of absence. Another failure.

After some time I pursued pharmacy school at D'Youville in Buffalo, New York. I've met new classmates, friends, and room-mates. The white coat ceremony was promising. However, a flashback to a previous memory. This led to many days of studying, clinical rotations, and connections. During this time I developed a new application, Vulture. It is an email social network. It is available on Amazon Appstore and GooglePlay. In addition, I produced merchandise that included clothes and apparel. Furthermore, I performed on the requirements of academic standards, but fell short the second year. In a state of disappoint, I'm encountering depression…

Story Volume 2
By
Earvin Phillip Eugene

Chapter 1: New Chapter

Friends always introduce you to new aspects of life. Their hobbies become your interests. Bonding through shared experiences is a great topic of discussion. One friend "Ray" has the habit of entertaining ladies of the night. He takes pleasure in searching through a catalog of women and starting a fun chat. Let's say slim women are his taste; all other characteristics seem to be secondary. They send back and forth reassuring messages to set a time and place. The whole process seems efficient. Myself being naïve to the whole experience for the most part, he was the teacher and I was the student. It can be strange since "Ray" was my junior. It always seems like all walks of life introduced me to something extreme rather than vice versa. As I had a sheltered upbringing. I provided a good ear and funny commentary in many relationships. Always making light of a situation.

"Ray" is Chinese and during conversations with him he described the ease and commonplace of this type of courting in China. Applications like WeChat and TanTan seem to be the proper channels of communication. He is funny and polite but can brag about his "accomplishments". There is a sense of organization and order against this madness. He digitally records and files his encounters with his partners. I joke that he is the Chinese version of "American Psycho". He would continue this habit in America, this was a new frontier to him. It is weird that he has a sleek physique with little to no facial or body hair, yet he acts on this vulgar tradition. You would not picture him as the culprit of this manly act. He is very skinny and has the routine of eating three big meals a day. It is safe to say he has a grand appetite. He works out in the evening before dinner with no gain in muscle. In the morning he applies many Asian products like facial cleansers to prevent acne and lighten his skin. He is always concerned about the emotions and thoughts of his girlfriend yet he really doesn't understand girls. We all have succumbed to his issue. Overall, he's a swell guy.

Chapter 2: More to Come

Trying to ease tensions of studies I spent time with friends, "Daniel" and "Justin". The two live together but do not have a transparent relationship. They have a strong friendship on the surface but independently disclose contrasting information about each other to me. Nonetheless, they are good people to shoot the shit. The one thing the two have in common are a pseudo sense of integrity and prowess as expected of people with political ambitions.

"Daniel" is the president of the student body government and has a military family background. He spent his adolescence in a Japanese naval base and has a cultural tattoo to show for it. He is fit and has an average level of intelligence. I will admit his glasses and confidence create a façade of knowledgeability. He enjoys going to hip-hop concerts and partakes in nicotine. Something we agree as good leisure. "Daniel" tends to lecture me in illicit prescriptions. It seems that anyone of a scientific background nowadays has tested drugs to prove its efficacy. He disclosed to me that he used to sell sorts of things to fund his ventures and school. The latter is respectable, but the former seemed to consume most of the expenses. The account appeared with a sense of privilege, yet some may argue that dealers are essential. "Justin" could not be aware of the actions of his beloved idol, "Daniel".

"Justin" is a fake social justice warrior. A follower of Bernie Sanders hoping to make his stand of today's civil rights movement for income inequality. He comes from an upper middle-class household, but at least he wants to spread the wealth. "Justin" follows all the latest trends like high socks, cardigan sweaters, and owning a vintage disk player. His time is spent at coffee shops, ambitious studying, and dating his long-term girlfriend. I have to admit "Justin" is more driven than "Daniel" but his personality is less appealing. He can be bland and strange, but at times persuasive. "Justin" shared to me his issues with health. He presented with some level of kyphosis and mentions his struggles with mental health. For about a year we were close and I supported him through times of trouble.

Chapter 3: Relationships

"Bella" was the girl next door who was looking to come out of her shell. She was the first girlfriend I truly cared for. "Bella" had long dark brown hair and light brown eyes. She possessed an amazing complexion and a bright smile. She had a sweet Italian mom and a fun Irish dad. Her mom has multiple sclerosis but was very vibrant and optimistic. "Bella" always told me her mom thought I was suitable for her. I was a hopeless romantic and, in my youth, I carried my heart on my sleeve. We both had an interest in music. She played for the school band and I had an upbringing in piano lessons. We had an innocent relationship of listening to music, playing Wii sports video games, watching movies, and walking through town. We would spend hours at my house bonding over every topic. My family supported that I developed a promising relationship with a good girl.

"Angel" was a lively and flirtatious girl. Her appearance was fit with strongly attractive features. "Angel" had a tan tone especially during the summer and small enough to truly grasp. She was the life of the party. She was up to my speed in the moment during ravishing times. Our relationship was private except amongst our friends. We would bring our friends together to party but on every occasion, we would escape to each other. We were inseparable at gatherings. Friends would joke on how attached we were to one another. So many inside jokes and private remarks we had of others. Our love was passionate and expressed at every moment. We were both in relationships with significant others at the time, so our meetings had to be concise. We would rendezvous at her place or my house with never a dull moment. Her room was interesting with mostly girly apparel. She was the type of girl to keep mementos of all the boys she loved before. Till' this day I hope I have a place in her heart. A sacred moment I hold dear to me is our late-night excursions in my family's pool. We always found a way to escape the responsibilities of the real world with one another.

Chapter 4: Family Ties

My cousin "John" is my closest confidant. He is tall and slim, hovering at 6 feet 4 inches. In his formative years he idolized Obama. He even went to Occidental College in Los Angeles, California to start a productive life. "John" started as a political science major and has always been well read on current topics. We always connected on business and news. I trust his opinions and I must mention he is one of the more intelligent figures in my life. He seeks guidance from me on pharmaceutical science and is the type of person that relies on plenty information before reaching a decision on many matters. However, he is stubborn at times and lacks true grit.

"John" started a college relationship with "Kate", which took him off his self-proclaimed path to success. By his accounts she was unruly and indifferent to many aspects of life. I can tell he cared for her during most parts of their relationship. It seemed that she troubled with drugs and addiction but concealed her dismay. He wanted to bring order to her life, but she wanted to be free. One day I met her at my cousin's house with my girlfriend at the time. She was quiet and timid. From what I have been told she is artistic studying film. I have no real opinion of her from our meeting. She was a girl of small stature with red hair. "Kate" possessed bright eyes and pale skin. I recall on that day we all shared of few drinks, played ping-pong, and pool. It was a short-lived night, but splendid. I appreciate the company of family and friends on most occasions.

My cousin would continue to graduate from Occidental College with a Bachelor's in Economics. We would celebrate with cigars at the harbor. We shared college experiences and discussed goals for the future. Our moments together fluctuate yet our connection never wavers. Blood is thicker than water.

Story Volume 3
By
Earvin Phillip Eugene

Chapter 1: Thoughts

"James" and I were close friends. James was an Italian American from an honest working-class family. His house was a home away from home. We shared Chinese food, watch classic movies like Pulp Fiction, and the basement smelled of teen spirit. I would invite girls and he would bring the recreational items. We were a grand duo, me being a social animal at the time and him laid back. "James" was a stocky fellow usually with a buzzcut. He played football for our high school until he developed some sort of "Metatarsus Adductus" (crooked foot). It was a permanent ailment and it is safe to say he self-medicated. Over the years he had a transformation of long brown curly hair and a laissez-faire attitude modeled after the counterculture movement of the 1960's.

Parties at his house were delightful. Friends and girls from around the Long Island town would join us. One time I spent a few hours in "James" brother bedroom with a lover. It was a night of great passion. When I took her home and arrived back to the party, my older brother and his girlfriend appeared. His girlfriend was best friends with my girlfriend, so my friends had to lie for my lack of judgement.

A party night that stands out was the one where I loss consciousness. I mixed too many party favors. It was a close call. I do not have much recollection of the event, but "James" made sure I was okay. Through this experience, I matured to monitor my intake. Today, I am a light drinker.

Chapter 2: Romance

"Amy" was a mature woman, but childish in her humor. She was what I needed at the time. Away from home, someone who was responsible, and kind was helpful. She has dyed blonde hair and brown eyes. We would watch Netflix, walk through the park, and attend the movies. Being with an older woman was a different experience for me. I enjoyed the time we spent together. She wanted the best for me. She always conveyed thoughts of ambition. I stayed motivated in graduate school and our time together was my release. Things became serious when she brought to my attention her cancer diagnosis. In order to illustrate my compassion, I introduced her to my family in Long Island. She would cook extravagant vegan meals. "Amy" is a great cook with a sophisticated menu. She introduced me to her niece, while they both stayed at my family home for part of the summer. My family accepted her. "Amy" and her family enjoyed the scenery of Long

Island at the Port Jefferson Harbor. She would return to Rhode Island and our relationship would end, but the time was well spent.

"Alexandra" is the apple of my eye. I met her when she was about nineteen. She is athletic and energetic. "Alexandra" ran track in high school and college. She went on to win many awards and accolades. Our relationship is very physical; however, it seems she always wanted more. She expects commitment from me, while enjoying life as a free spirit. Her immaturity was evident, but she is blossoming to an attractive and independent woman. We have an on and off relationship even to this day. She has met my family and we all see her promise. One of the first moments we spent time together, she wanted to twerk on Snapchat. Today, she is studying science at Syracuse University. I appreciate her thoughts and beauty, but I am unaware on how to manage her. If it is meant to be, it will be.

Chapter 3: Companion

"Benjamin" is my longest lasting friend. He is of Italian and Jewish descent at the height of 6'1. We toked together, played soccer together, and spent time with girls together. He is good people. "Benjamin" was always a better driver than me, so he would take the wheel. He currently works for the United States Postal Service. I recall one time when we were in high school, I would take him home from school. It was a snowy and icy day. I crashed my Nissan onto his neighbor's lawn. The neighbor and "Benjamin" helped me clear the car free. My parents do not know of my mistake until this day.

My friend even hooked up with my girl at the time, "Jasmine". She was an open-minded girl that was promiscuous. I appreciate the respect he had to tell me of their encounter. It was not strange for us to have a bond with a same girl. Within the past year we took a trip to an Islanders game. I am glad he is still in good spirits.

Chapter 4: Travels

I remember one family road trip down the Atlantic coast. From New York to Florida. The car of choice was a Ford minivan. Being small at the time, it was a house on wheels. Me, my older brother and younger sister brought pillows and covers. My parents disgruntledly played hip-hop of the 2000's for us. As they preferred classics like Marvin Gaye, Whitney Houston, and the like. I played with my revolutionary PSP, while staring at the changing geography. My brother and sister were into the music as they still enjoy it today. When they fell asleep, I was just in awe of my parents. So jubilant to be a part of the family with the safety and protection away from the outside world.

It was the typical American trip to Disney World. It was a wonder land. Seeing all my cartoons come to life was unimaginable. Disney channel and movies were very popular at the time. The tropical atmosphere and sunny days were different to me. We would spend time with my uncle, Marc who is a flight surgeon for the U.S. Air Force that lives in Florida. Also, my grandparents spend great deal of time in Florida as well. It was a reunion. Especially, since most of my infant years was when I enjoyed my grand-parents company.

Another family vacation was to Las Vegas, Nevada. The ideal location for a pubescent young teenager. This time the trip was in the air. Flights are an important experience to see the world past by in the skies. Sin city was a hot desert during the day and cool at night. It was mystical to see the bright city at night surrounded by vast emptiness. Seeing adults in their playground was adventurous. We saw the Blue Man Group and amazing magic tricks. I was blinded by the lights and glamour.

The trip to the ocean on Royal Caribbean was a different experience. There is nothing like spending time in the sea, island hopping between countries. I was amused with the pool and basketball court on board and each tour of an island. We would see Jamaica, Grand Cayman Islands, and so forth. My brother being older would sneak into the clubs on board. One night he managed to engage with an older woman. I witnessed the event. It was nice climbing the hills of Jamaica. Smelling the fresh air. Walking through the beaches of the Grand Cayman Islands. Water clearer than I ever seen before.

Jaded
By
Earvin Phillip Eugene

Chapter 1: Commencement

Jordan Williams attended Dartmouth college. He worked at Zimmerman Fitness Center. Jordan needed the money and it was his opportunity to meet colleagues. He was about 5'11, brown-skinned with short black curly hair. Jordan sported glasses as he was near-sighted and groomed himself with a goatee. He wore outlandish fashion with striking designs such as a red and black flannel sweatshirt alongside checkered pants. On some days he would dress in Dartmouth green apparel, but today was a special day. Jordan had to spend time with his girlfriend, Mae, it was there one-year anniversary.

Jordan was walking through campus passing by the "Dartmouth Green" on his way to School House where he resides. His room was simple with a desk and bed. He had vintage posters of the Beatles and Muhammad Ali. He was a "classic man". Atop of his bed was a Ghana flag as his parents were immigrants and he was first generation African American. He was proud of his ancestry; being 41% Ghana, 25% Cameroon-Congo, 10% British (Anglo-Saxon), 10% Benin-Togo, 3% French, 2% Nigerian, 2% Greece-Albanian, 2% Portuguese, 2% Senegal, 2% Irish Celtic, and 1% Slavic as reported by AncestryDNA. As many other black people, he was unaware of his diverse cultural background but was curious to trace his roots.

The quad was placed with four roommates including Jordan, Alex, I.T., and Asim. Alex Fischer was a first generation American with his parents from Romania. He grew up in Newtown, Connecticut. Alex was smaller in stature, with a height of 5'6. He had dark brown hair and bright green eyes. Alexander exercised frequently and followed a specific diet regimen. He only ate fruits and vegetables during the week. He majored in business and was more of a serious fellow. Jordan told Alex "let's drink a few beers and watch The Killing of a Sacred Deer on Netflix". Alex agreed and said, "why not". It was Friday and it was routine for them to relax from a rough week. Jordan believed this gave him enough time to unwind before Mae would arrive in the evening. Alex used to be a party animal in the beginning of college, but now became more studious and reserved. Jordan believed ritually in drinking to share fun moments.

Jordan studied biology with a minor in writing. He was a renaissance man. His goal is to become a scientific writer for the Food & Drug Administration. His family advising him to go into medicine like his uncles. Jordan stated "Martin" from The Killing of a Sacred Deer was "creepy, something is off about him." Alex found entertainment in "Steven Murphy" sex scene with his wife "Anna". Alex proclaimed, "Nicole Kidman is hot!" They both laughed and agreed. Alex continued to simultaneously work on school assignments and surf the internet on his laptop as he watched the movie. Jordan decided to have a few more Keystone beers. He became noticeably drunk. Alex did not mind; he enjoyed the company instead of his usual solitude.

Mae arrived at the door. Jordan is quite functional drunk; except he becomes slightly sloppy with his actions and motives. He rejoiced to open the door and see Mae. He declared his affection for her by giving a strong hug and saying, "How are you baby?" She showed disapproval of his state by accepting the hug, but not returning it. She stated, "What are we going to do for our anniversary?" Mae has always been straightforward, Jordan liked that about her. He was amused by her frustration against her petite physique. Jordan smiled and said, "We could go to a frat party at Alpha Chi Alpha." She agreed. Mae went to the refrigerator and began to drink a Keystone beer. They were past the nights of strong liquor at dorm parties from their freshman years and started to broaden their horizons at frat parties. There were things to do and people to meet on campus nowadays. Mae walked to Jordan's bedroom away from the common area to talk as Jordan prepared for their night out. She used to play soccer in high school, which explained her slim and athletic appearance. It also provided her confidence from being a team leader. Her childhood consisted of traveling across the country in tournaments with teammates and her parents. Mae was very knowledgeable but not the ambitious type academically in her youth. It was a way of revolting from her father, a reputable biology professor at Stony Brook University. Her resume was salvaged with plenty of extracurricular activities. Including the fact, she had guidance from her dad to attend Stony Brook University. See, Mae's education was at Stony Brook Preparatory High School and Jordan at Ward Melville High School. Two neighboring schools on Long Island, New York. In fact, that is how they met at a joint high school party one Summer senior year. They dated but had a long-distance relationship for some time. Mae at Stony Brook University for Freshman and Sophomore year before transferring to Dartmouth. And Jordan spending his complete time there. It was a matter of time before their combined efforts would place them together. It was not enough to see each other during the offseason of college. Mae mentioned a good poem from Rupi Kaur of "Milk and Honey" and described new hip-hop songs she heard from "The Weeknd". Jordan interestingly listened, while looking at her light brown eyes with freckles. She played with her dark brown hair as he finished getting ready.

Asim entered the dorm. He was of average height and build. His family was of Indian descent. He was personable and a fair-minded person. Asim was Muslim in faith and therefore did not drink alcohol. This was different from most of the Dartmouth student body. However, he did vape and preferred hookah when given the opportunity. Alex said, "What's up bud?" Asim stated, "Bro I just got a blitzy (Blitzmail) from lips (Amy)". They called her lips simply for the characteristic of her full lips. She was a mixed beauty of Asian and Hispanic heritage. All the guys in School House wanted to spend time with her. Alex was not surprised and said, "She wants you dude, what did she say?" Asim spoke aloud, "These are the lips, powerful rudders pushing through groves of kelp, this girl's terrible, unsweetened taste of the whole ocean, its fathoms: *this is that taste*." Jordan entered the common area and proclaimed, "Lips is aware of her lips" and laughed. Mae stated "you guys are stupid, Asim I think you two are a good match. I can put in a good word for you." As she reached in the fridge for one more Keystone. Asim started inhaling from his Juul and mentioned his satisfaction. Alex would play "Reckless" by Arin Ray on YouTube on the Smart TV to set the pregame mood as he finished his beer. He rejoiced "Asim's got it made". Jordan began to take a few puffs from Asim's vape and stated, "Alex good choice". They would all continue with banter alongside different fun and melodic music. Vaping and drinking beers until about 9:30 at night when Jordan stated, "We better head out." In a calm and friendly manner, Jordan and Mae left the dorm. Alex and Asim went to their separate rooms.

Chapter 2: Party Favor

It was Springtime in Hanover, New Hampshire. The weather was cool on this night. Much warmer than the difficult Winters. Jordan and Mae enjoyed the fresh air of New England. The Alpha Chi Alpha party was full of vibrant faces and excited individuals. The house had a pungent smell of stale beer. Music was loud and energetic. It was Dartmouth tradition to play beer pong without the handle of the paddle. It was a fun twist to the game. Jordan being a Senior had the experience to play along with other Seniors. Mae was his partner on the table, and they were a great duo.

Later in the night, full of drunken spirit the two wanted to sober up and find time alone. They made it just in time to the Pine for a quick meal. They had the Grab N' Go that included cheeseburger and fries. They usually preferred the Courtyard Café, but tonight was a special occasion. On the way back to School House, Jordan gave Mae a Pandora charm bracelet. She embraced him with a kiss. In the moment she was full of bliss. Girls like things. This gift would buy her affection for at least a week. Mae was thankful, but accustomed to receiving gifts.

They arrived back at School House and ate their food enjoying the quietness. It was a sincere moment between two lovers. After the meal, Jordan asked Mae, "Do you love me?" She answered, "I do." They went to the bedroom and began to undress. Mae was beautiful naked with subtle freckles and tan skin. Jordan with his strong shape, grabbed her and they made love.

Once they finished, Mae rested her head onto Jordan's chest for quite some time. Mae got dressed as they both had few inhalations of Jordan's vape. She left into the night. Once alone with his thoughts, Jordan went through his stash and found his half-finished bottle of Chairman's Reserve Rum. He received it during a past family trip to St. Lucia. He took a few swigs to end the night. After all, today was a day of celebration.

In the morning, Jordan followed his typical routine of vaping and drinking tea. He was met by his roommate I.T., he must have arrived at some point last night. I.T. was a Nigerian whose name stood for Ifedolapo Tijani. He was six feet tall right on the nose. Tall and dark-skinned with unmatched white bright teeth. He was plainly muscular with little effort to exercise or conditioning. He possessed an accent and was the most mature of the group. I.T. stated, "You have fun last night?" Jordan in a joking manner, "It was the time of my life." Tijani shared political commentary on politics and Trump. He mostly described satire of the president suggesting administering disinfectants like Lysol and Clorox to treat Coronavirus infections. Jordan was amused and mentioned how Trump is the funniest president ever.

The discussion became more serious when Jordan explained he needed to get something off his chest. He began to describe the night a few weeks ago when he attended a party at Kappa Kappa Kappa with his friend Jared. They competed for this pretty and captivating girl. Jordan made a pass at her, commenting on the fact that "She was not one for emptying her face of expression." Her face was evenly symmetric and resembled a lively Logan Laurice Browning. She brought him to a private room for what Jordan thought would be a romantic linkage. However, she described to him of his wrongdoing in praising women solely on their physical appearance. He was distraught and responded by saying "I want to get to know you." The girl stated, "I am not the type of girl for you" and kissed him on the cheek. This left Jordan more fascinated by her. Jared would have several failed attempts at the girl before they both surrendered.

Jordan felt guilty in his aspirations of girls while still being in a long-lasting relationship. I.T. reassured him of all men's shortcomings in this matter. He said "You're young, but you love her" regarding Mae. Jordan simply agreed. In order to ease tension, he illustrated how the frat party host placed dirty socks in the alcohol punch bowl before the gathering and advised him with caution to drink on that night. It is safe to say, Jordan only drank from Keystone beer cans. Ifedolapo laughed and said, "only at Dartmouth".

Chapter 3: Hiatus

It was Spring Break and Jordan was back on Long Island. He spent time with his childhood friend Joseph. They would go to his basement and smoke "Blue Dream" from the bong. This became their recreation ever since they both graduated high school. They played FIFA on the Xbox. Jordan was better at the game than Joseph, but it was just a means to pass time. Joseph prided himself on being a good host. He mixed some Long Island Iced Teas and shared stories from the past. Whether it be, Joseph's past prowess as a football player or the times they both attended their school's county lacrosse games yearly at Stony Brook University. It was good to be back home.

Joseph's older brother, Matthew, was visiting from New Jersey and arrived in the basement for greetings. He hovered over the two. Tall in stature. He was a funny and athletic fellow. Matthew announced, "What's up pussies?" and took part in the festivities. In customary fashion, he bragged of his past achievements. Whether it be about the women he managed to conquer or the championships from lax. He beat Jordan in FIFA and reminded him of his years of experience with the game. Matthew represented the relic of the "Long Island Bro". He mentioned to them his bachelor's party arrangement because he was to be married to his longtime girlfriend and fiancé. The two brothers discussed the savage time they would have in Atlantic City to celebrate. There would be girls, gambling, and cocaine. Jordan had to go back to school for graduation, so he could not make it. In addition, he never did anything pass weed. Joseph being more experienced proposed Jordan try magic mushrooms, "it's a life changing opportunity." They decided for Joe to buy the stuff so Jordan could give it a try.

Certain plans changed when Jordan wished to try shrooms with Mae. They determined it was best to do it in an open serene place. Mae suggested Avalon Park in old historic Stony Brook. Mae was skeptical in trying psychedelic drugs, just like Jordan she only experimented with marijuana. She recalled the time Jordan and she had brownies and thought it would be similar. They laughed and cried tears of joy. Mae was open-minded and she could not think of a better thing to do with her boyfriend on Spring Break.

It was a bright sunny day and all the flowers were blooming at Avalon. The scenery was very versatile. It started at a bridge that mimicked a Japanese garden. There was a beautiful arrangement of sparkling colors. The water underneath the bridge had synchronous waves with the wind as if the earth itself was breathing. Next, followed the stone steps. Hard and very symmetric. Above reached a replica ritual circle from some ancient civilization. It was composed of stone and grass. In the past the two took for granted the spiritual representation of the site. After, they reached what appeared to imitate farmland. Yellow wheatgrass flowed around the dirt path. They truly felt isolated as it seemed few people were on the path today. There was a sense of excitement and pleasure mixed against melancholy. Stumbling through the majestic path, they arrived at tranquil shrubbery. The environment was lush green and at the center a blue pond. Colors like on a canvas were noticeable throughout the surrounding. In the moment there was bliss. Jordan and Mae absorbed the animals and nature. They decided to go back to the entrance. Time felt as it was rewinding as the two held hands for reassurance walking back. By the gateway it seemed as if the roads were slowly oscillating. The pavement appeared to have dramatic humps. In a state of panic Jordan and Mae rushed into his car. Sitting in the backseat, a British police officer strolled past as something seen from a stereotypical image on Google. He wore a bobby on the beat and held an old school Billy Club. They were shocked. A few steps behind the officer was a brown man of Sikh faith. They were in awe of what they were seeing. It could not be possible. In order to calm down they stared at their iPhones. The devices possessed magical pixel colors. Mae suggested they get fresh air outside the car when the coast seemed clear. They felt calmer. Jordan and Mae viewed each other. Mae said, "You look stunning." She described how he looked so young and high-spirited. His skin was shiny and clear of blemishes. As Jordan looked at Mae, he stated, "You look remarkable!" Apparently, each brown strand of hair was noticeable. He could imagine her as an old woman and she still seemed beautiful. Still high, they discussed driving back to Jordan's home to end this escapade. Mae was determined to drive Jordan's car nervously. She forcibly stated, "Jordan the reality of the situation is you are black, and I don't want you to get arrested for driving under the influence." Jordan was upset but did not feel this was the time and place to have an enduring argument of the complexities of racial injustice in America, so he receded. Mae drove, as they were still tripping. They arrived safe and sound at Jordan's house. They were relieved. His parents were watching television. Mae and Jordan, he heated up a frozen pizza and went to Jordan's room. He was impressed by her courage. The exchanged remarks about the whole experience. They ate the pizza, which seemed more delicious than usual. Jordan kissed Mae, and they made love with the remnants of the high. The sex was more caring compared to other times.

Chapter 4: Convocation

It was time for graduation. Everyone on campus was covered in green and black caps and gowns. Alex and Jordan sneaked cigarettes by the campus in the morning. Sometimes there is no substitute for the real thing. Jordan sprayed himself with Polo Red by Ralph Lauren cologne to hide his misbehavior. He shared a few shots of his rum with I.T. and Alex, as Asim drank Red bull and vaped at the dorm.

They each discussed what they would do after graduation. Alex would apply to be a consultant with his economics degree at Bain Capital in Boston, Massachusetts. He mentioned an alumnus of the firm, "Mitt Romney made it there, so can I". Asim, who studied Political Science and Government, would become a public policy analyst before tossing his hat in the ring at law school, preferably, Columbia University. Ifedolapo as a computer science engineer had his sights set at Google. Finally, Jordan with mixed feelings from his passion and family pressure believed he would take a year off to travel and drink. Realistically, he knew that he would work with his family's support until he was ready to apply to medical school. This depressed him. He made a cheer to the future with his friends.

The ceremony was splendid. All his close ones were present. His father, mother, older brother, and younger sister were all there to witness his success. Mae and her family were in attendance as well. Mae with her psychology background would work under her father and perhaps take a children's psychologist job in the meantime before applying to medical school to become a psychiatrist. Her father wanted his daughter to have the interactive skills of a professor, while the lucrative position of a doctor.

The guest speaker spoke of perseverance and ambition in life. The possibilities for the future being endless. A quote from Dr. Seuss stroke attention, "You're off to Great Places! Today is your day! Your mountain is waiting, So... get on your way!" The calling of names for diplomas would ensue. Jordan, Mae, and all their friends received mentions. Everyone was ecstatic and grateful. One of Jordan's favorite professors stated, "Don't cry because it's over. Smile because it happened" and handed him a fine cigar. The moment was profound.

Upon returning to Long Island for the Summer, Jordan met with his cousin to drink and smoke cigars at the harbor to celebrate. He too just graduated UCLA with a bachelor's in history. They roamed around the area puffing their tobacco. James, his cousin, discussed the last great American president was Kennedy. To evade the Cuban Missile Crisis, help the disenfranchised during the Civil Rights era, and the fact that he intellectualized international and domestic affairs at the ripe age of forty-three years old.

The two entered the Brewology bar at Port Jefferson, this time Jordan shared scientific facts about ethanol metabolism. He described how alcohol is degraded by an enzyme called alcohol dehydrogenase. The alcohol is changed to acetaldehyde, next to acetate, and finally into carbon dioxide and water. He paraphrased that ethanol is the intoxicating part of alcohol and as it reaches the brain, it interferes with normal neurotransmission. Jordan said, "Here's to alcohol, the rose-colored glasses of life" with a smile. That day was especially good, so he thought.

Jordan ended the evening by spending time with Mae at West Meadow Beach. Usually, the place was delightful, many great memories were shared there, however in this occasion it felt somber. She had bad news. Mae told Jordan she was pregnant. Jordan stayed calm and said, "We'll take care of it". Mae cried, but knew it was best. She was upset but realized she was not alone in the matter. This would be the most difficult part of their relationship with constant bickering and slight comments. Deep down they knew the real issue was the unborn child, but it was not something they had the maturity to debate. The two resolved the problem in the coming week, so they thought. After the ordeal, the partnership was never the same. Whether it be due to the nerve-wrecking and painful process of an abortion or because they felt what was the point of a relationship that did not lead to family and marriage. Within a few months, the relationship met its end.

Without the support of a loving companion and the pressures of the world after graduation Jordan confided in the bottle. He drank strong liquor at home. Sometimes friends would stop by to hangout and family encouraged him to be productive, but nobody knew his pain. One night fueled by sleep deprivation, sadness, and drunkenness he started a heated argument with his family. His parents and siblings were scared for Jordan's health with nothing left to do they provided police and ambulance support to take him to the hospital.

Chapter 5: Not Oneself

Psychiatric emergency at the hospital was a place unknown to Jordan. As he sobered up, he was alarmed and worried. The staff provided him Ativan to calm his nerves. Jordan had to strip down to his underwear and was observed for physical harm or any potential weapons. He dressed himself in scrubs and had to spend several nights with other patients. Some were criminals and others were deranged. Healthcare professionals viewed them from a safe and protective barrier, only contacting them to administer medications or perform quick psych evaluations. During his stint at the emergency hospital he got involved in an altercation with another patient. A guy tried to push Jordan around because he stood out like a sore thumb, several patients for some reason or another disliked him. They de-escalated the situation and injected Jordan with drugs. In a drowsy state, he walked to his hospital bed and knowing he would soon be unconscious. He was left in a haze of security, doctors, and nurses attending to him.

Jordan was transported to a behavioral psych and rehabilitation center. It was different than anything he was accustomed to but there was a strict regimen. The daily routine consisted of smoking in the gated courtyard, breakfast with medications, recreation, lunch, entertainment and counseling, dinner with medications and another smoke break. It was a glance into the real world. Patients were homeless taking advantage of the system they were given, entitled people with a dysfunctional background like Jordan, and in general individuals down on their luck. One thing they all had in common was they all were suffering in one form or another. On his first night, a bum offered him alcohol in which he managed to sneak into the premises. If Jordan were not about his wits and truly attempting to make a change in his life, he would have indulged.

In the morning, a cigarette to adjust to his new setting. Surprisingly, a healthy breakfast with eggs, milk, and fruit. Drugs that altered his mind and thoughts, presumably for the better. A short time of television in the common area, in which the seniors controlled the channels. There was a hierarchy of the patients at the hospital. Those who not only suffered from mental illness but performed some criminal acts on the outside or were simply strong in figure to demand authority. The true power lied with the healthcare professionals who could command rule with the force of security disguised as aides. If you fell from favor of the doctors or nurses, one could be subjected to an injection for bad behavior. Jordan did his best to stay calm and focused. For recreation, he kept a journal to track his thoughts, daily occurrences, and possible improvements in his actions. For lunch, he planned with the dietician to have salads. One of the patients who was ignorant to the guidelines to adjust his diet with the nutritionist was upset to see Jordan eating a salad and he spit on him from across the cafeteria. The aides detained him as the nurses injected him with a mixture of Depakote and Ativan for his misbehavior and he was left to rest in his room. Before counseling, he talked on the phone with his parents. They ensured him to stay strong and to continue with the treatment.

At counseling, the psychiatrist and social worker described to him that he suffers from depression and schizophrenia. They came to this conclusion since Jordan did not keep the best hygiene during his stay. His facial hair was unmanaged, displaying an unkept beard. His nails were not as clean as usual. He presented with delusions that people at the hospital disliked him. Jordan said, "I'm piece of shit." The doctor privately consoled to him that he reminded him of his son and reassured him that things will get better in time.

After dinner, one of the patients, who was short but strong physically played chess with him. Jordan soundly won at the game and the patient became furious. The patient forced him into the hallway and punched him in the gut. The patient was attacked and detained. He was medicated and stripped himself naked on his hospital bed before he was tied down. He was unconscious with an erection on the bed. Obviously, the patient was ill and possessed a sick sense of humor. Much of the staff were amused and laughed. The men were glad that he was obstructed, and the women were appalled. Jordan relaxed for a short period of time in the recreational area and reflected. Jordan smoked his cigarette, took his medications, and slept the night away.

Most days at the center were the same. Jordan's parents visited more often over time to check on his development. He prepared to leave, and one kind patient gave him the shirt on his back for good fortune. One nurse gave remarks of how much she is going to miss Jordan. All he could think of how far he came. He was hopeful for the future, but he was jaded.

Everybody Loves You But Nobody Likes You
By
Earvin P Eugene

Chapter 1: Place

In this Los Angeles ledge house resides Samuel Pierre. A modern art design home with unique faces. It was surrounded by a small forest with a stone path leading to the steps of his dwelling. Temperate climate and bright sun made the area captivating. Presented inside were white walls filled with portraits of extravagant paintings. Artwork resembling "Café Terrace at Night" and "Nighthawks" by Edward Hopper. The space had a huge spread, larger than it would seem from the outside. In his office lied books from the past. Varying subjects, such as "War & Peace", "This Side of Paradise", and no good home can exist safely without the bible. The office was filled with clean furnished wood. This was his place of solitude. In the living room there was his big smart television at the center, a comfortable couch, a few chairs, and to the side a shelf filled with scripts and screenplays. In the city of angels, it was only right for Sam to be a Hollywood writer. On the shelf were works he wrote and developed like "Story" and "Jaded". And others of idols like Quentin Tarantino's "Once Upon A Time in Hollywood", Jordan Peele's "Get Out", and Martin Scorsese's "The Wolf of Wall Street". The kitchen was simple and nice with a black granite island and counters. In the silver fridge were fruits and vegetables, but mostly Devil's Spring Vodka. Sam kept them cold to make the drinks more palatable. There were two bathrooms at the residence. One of which was spectacular possessing black marble at all corners. A sauna and jacuzzi for entertainment. A shower with an area to sit and all possible water pressures. A heating red light and complete ceiling with a mirror to witness his dirty acts of pleasure. The other bathroom was heavenly with white design everywhere. Inside, the sun would shine through mosaic glass. A white porcelain jacuzzi stood in the corner. The shower had clear glass and clean corners. Finally, the master bedroom was something from MTV Cribs. A king size bed where the magic happened with red velvet sheets. Black carpets, a television, and a walk-in closet. Two windows with massive curtains. His favorite part was a doorway that led to a balcony.

Chapter 2: Reflection

Samuel was sitting in the living room drinking the vodka. The TV was white noise as he dreamed of another time. He remembered the family trip he took to Mexico when he was about twelve years old. He was with his dad, mom and siblings. The weather was hot and sunny in the Summer. It was tropical with natural beauty. He past the rural towns, there was blatant poverty on the way to the resort. Sam recalled how upset that made him. He felt helpless and never wanted to experience it himself, perhaps that is what motivated him to be the success he is today. Samuel did not understand how the people could still be hopeful with the cards they were dealt. The poor natives were all happy with a strong community that appreciated a fine connection between family and friends. The area was fruitful for what seemed likes miles of vegetation and natural resources.

At the resort, Sam's family went jet skiing, snorkeling, and scuba diving in blue clear waters. One day he almost drowned swimming. He could not breathe, and he was disappearing to infinite darkness. It was a scary time that felt like lasted hours. A resort worker saved him. He was lucky. Young Sam was grateful. At that moment he wished that at any bad point in his life that someone would save him.

Now starting the second bottle of Devil's Spring, he floated in and out of consciousness. Samuel haphazardly walked upstairs to the bedroom. He rested on the soft bed and attempted to watch YouTube on his laptop. It was no use, with a few more gulps, he was off contemplating about a memory from the past.

Mister Pierre in high school was a somewhat popular fellow. He spent time with the jocks, nerds, and stoners. Never choosing sides, he enjoyed the company of interesting classmates. Awkward and young at the time, he talked to this ordinary girl online without barely conversing with her in-person. From the guidance of his friends, they advised him to talk to as many girls as possible to find a match. One was bound to stick. This girl eventually would come over his house to hook up. In his basement, they shared small talk about school and music as they watched a movie. The two kissed and he felt her supple breasts. Sam wanted to take it a step further, but the girl stopped his proceedings. She explained, "I do not really do this." No harm no foul, he valued their time together and they talked for a few weeks before cutting ties.

In immature fashion, he talked to the girl's friend, Cara. They communicated sparingly. Eventually, his brother partied with her. During the event in a drunken blur she performed fellatio on him. In the ensuing days, Sam's brother gloated about the interaction with Cara. Out of spite, Samuel invited Cara to their house when his brother was away at work. Sam and Cara drank some beer. She asked of Sam's brother whereabouts, he replied "He's not around." That evening, Sam and Cara had sex. He was quite satisfied of his decision and never told his older brother of the occurrence.

Chapter 3: Resolution

Samuel Pierre finished the bottle. He walked to the balcony. Now, he had no idea where he was. The world was spinning. Again, for the final time he stood with poor balance and thought about something old. He fell forward over the ledge.

BUM
By
Earvin Eugene

Chapter 1: Clouded Judgement

In a room full of smoke were Evan and Mia. They were in Evan's bedroom. Mia never got high before. Evan prided himself as a connoisseur of bud. The weed was green with bright yellow hairs and had a pungent smell. In New York, it is common to possess sour diesel. They used a small glass bong, which Evan bought from a friend. He got it for a fair price, and it could even store ice for cool smoke. The two colored the device with rainbow hearts as this was their project. With a few inhalations, they laughed at Rick & Morty and BoJack Horseman cartoons. They sanitized the room with Ozium spray as they hid underneath the bed sheets. As the air cleared, Evan said, "This is the best time of my life". Mia stated, "So, this is what being high is like." It was a feeling of euphoria, a soothing sense for a good day, and with the good stuff no paranoia. Blood rushes to the brain and results in a clarity of vision.

On another occasion Evan and Mia tried pot brownies. Their attitude was something from a Cheech and Chong movie. Whatever happens, happens. The chocolate desert tasted delicious with no hint of the plant. Mia questioned how long it would take to kick in. Evan with the experience to have done it with a past girlfriend said, "It should take about forty-five minutes to feel something." The sensation was a bodily high. They felt sensitive to the world. The material of their clothes and the bed felt tremendously soft. There was bliss in feeling the gradual high. The peak was miraculous. The epitome of relaxed and ecstatic. Mia said, "I don't do drugs. I set plants on fire and breathe." That was enough to make both laugh for five minutes. The come down was magnificent, bringing the imaginary and real world together.

Evan resembled a modern-day Jimi Hendrix, skinny with a miniature afro. Wearing vibrant tie dye hippie sweatshirts. In fact, his favorite quote was "Please pass me the peace weed and take some heed. Throw all that mixed up speed." His favorite pastime was enjoying a few bong hits, playing soccer with friends, and traveling when he could afford it. He believed toking on a bong was the cleanest way to get high. He rarely drank alcohol except socially at parties. His worst habit was smoking beedis during his tour through the Caribbean. It was cheap and addictive. He felt that marijuana relieved many addictions to other substances. Evan was a straightforward young man who enjoyed the simple things in life. His wildest action was getting a small tattoo on his inner bicep, "It Was Always You" from the Great Gatsby. He helped around the house to support his family when he could and his major task was walking his dog, Buddy, around the neighborhood park or downtown. Evan loved buddy and raised him since he was a puppy. Buddy was a poodle, protective, smart, and loyal. The two were inseparable.

Mia was a look alike of Miley Cyrus. Short blonde hair and blue eyes. She was more experienced than Evan in the tattoo department, having a heart tattoo on her wrist and a flower on her inner thigh. She was clever and partied a lot. She liked film and worked at a café. Mia enjoyed the arts, and even had a hobby of drawing interesting things from serene photos. Evan would take the photos and Mia would draw. It was a match made in heaven.

Chapter 2: Abandonment

High school had come to an end, and it was time for Evan to have more discipline at least that is what his parents thought. They would antagonize him for being "lazy" and "ungrateful". Soon, they realized he was smoking marijuana as Evan became sloppy in covering his tracks. The family was constantly at odds. One fight escalated to the point where Evan had to leave the house. He packed his belongings and took the car to his cousins. At first, he was greeting with open arms. His father communicated with his uncle and discussed his disapproval. Regardless, his uncle let him stay for a short period of time. Evan would perform chores like buying groceries, taking out the trash, and help cook whatever he could. Eventually, the family grew tired of his smoking habits. Pressuring him to quit and make something of his life. He was puzzled on how to be better. A lot of his family was conservative when it came to pot. One day, when his uncle was away at work, Evan and his cousin, Josh smoked weed in his treehouse. Josh used to smoke weed away at school and his parents were upset with his choices as well. Josh's plan was to switch to a more respectable vice, like drinking. He advised Evan to do the same. In the coming days, Josh drank in the evenings as Evan continued to smoke weed. His cousin's family grew tired of him and kicked him out. Josh was upset, "Stop smoking in my house" and slapped Evan in the face. He threw his stuff on the front lawn and they demanded he returned home to his parents. Josh would become an alcoholic. Perhaps, the plant is better than the drink, who is to say.

Evan now on his own again took the car to his friend's house, Rahman. He was older and rented a house with his girlfriend. Evan confided in Rahman of his disdain for his family. Rahman advised him to be patient and things would calm down. He reminded him that Evan's family cared for him. It was tough love. Evan lit up a joint in the backyard and pondered on how things went astray. He could not pinpoint a solution to his problem. Now, stoned in a better mood, he battled his munchies by raiding through Rahman's fridge for whatever was not wanted. That night, Evan relaxed on the couch, scrolling through his iPhone but heard what sounded like Rahman making love to his girlfriend. Evan thought of Mia and texted her. She gave him advice to stay optimistic and that they should get place together out west in Colorado. Evan was enamored by the idea, but it seemed to difficult to bring to actualization. Rahman was a great host but soon he too grew tired of Evan "stinking" up the house with weed smoke. Rahman was less forceful but threw shade on Evan every time he saw him. Eventually, Rahman's girlfriend had a heated argument with him for Evan to leave. It was about that time. Evan told Rahman, "We'll talk soon" as he grabbed his stuff and left.

The next stop was to his childhood friend's house, Ralph. He too was a stoner, so what is the worst that could happen, thought Evan. Evan even bought weed from Ralph from time to time. Both smoked weed until their eyes turned red on most nights. It was splendid. Ralph would work at the local bagel store during the day and they would toke up at night. Mia would visit sometimes have a puff or two and check that Evan was doing okay. She said privately to Evan, "We can make it out there". He hesitantly kissed her and agreed. It was the dream to smoke and eat great food, while watching the best films from Aaron Sorkin (The Social Network) and Spike Lee (Blackkklansman) but time was running out. For the first time, Evan felt like he was wasting time at a month's end. He decided there was no better time than now to leave with Mia.

Chapter 3: The Great Escape

Evan met Mia at Ralph's house. The two had their bags packed. He stared at her, she was like a child to him, and stated "Let's do this together and not look back". She showed him a picture of their life together in the future on her phone. It was a solemn drawing of Evan smoking a joint with Mia and a baby in front of a nice house by a picket fence. Evan took a dub bag from Ralph got in his dad's car that he has been roaming with and left with Mia on their way out West. They believed with a little weed and love you could make it in America.

May 11th
Subtitle: Jeanine
By
Earvin P Eugene

Chapter 1: Young Lady

May 11th marks the day of the passing of my grandmother, Jeanine Eugene. She was born in Haiti, with mixed blood and the passion of a true Caribbean. I imagine her spending days in the sun at the beach, reading books, and listening to the radio. She grew up in a more prosperous time in Haiti under Papa Doc. Although the regime was totalitarian, basic goods of commerce and electricity were available. People could enjoy the simple pleasures of life on an island, such as swimming, eating fruits, and attending festivals if they abided by certain rules. Knowing my grandma during the later parts of her life, I witnessed her caring heart, leadership of the family, and compassion to provide for those less fortune. Remembering her in the best possible light, she must have been the apple of the eye to my grandpa. They must have labored in the hot sun during the day and partied the night away.

Picture Jeanine and Reynold (grandpa) in Port-au-Prince, Haiti struggling in an impoverished nation but hoping for more. A man from the countryside mountains and a woman from urban life meeting in a small country. Attempting to enjoy what little they had and with the ambition to improve their lives. My grandma must have won my grandpa's heart with food. At the time women prided themselves on the preparation of extravagant meals. My grandma being a great cook, would make Griot, Kibi, Lalo Legume, and on special holidays like New Years, Joumou squash soup. They must have shared great thoughts and expressed love for one another. Youthful bliss was cut short as the case with many people during hard times. They would start a family, go to the United States, and send money back to their children living in Haiti.

Chapter 2: Wife & Mother

My grandma would have five sons and one daughter. All of whom needed my grandparents support in their childhood, adolescence, and early adulthood. The dream was for them to later come to New York and improve their lives. The goal of every generation is for the next to live a better life. Jeanine and Reynold were situated in the poor neighborhood of East New York City (Brooklyn) during the 1970's and 1980's. You could imagine the infestation of drug and crime during this era. New to the country they were petrified and learned the hustle and bustle of New York. They lived in a small apartment, working countless hours during the day. Jeanine being a nurse and Reynold being a factory worker. The laboring days were long and treacherous. Both did the best that they could with what they had. Being from a small tropical island, the winters were difficult to endure, and their living space was poor. However, only in America could they make any amount of substantial money as Haiti lacked self-reliance with poverty and nationwide corruption.

My grandparents would soon send for my father, uncles, and aunt. The living space would become tighter and less manageable. A complete family now lived in such small living quarters. My father loved my grandma and did his best to make her life more pleasant and safe. He would work small jobs, parking cars in garages and performing deliveries to help pay rent and food costs. My father would take Jeanine to train and bus stops to prevent danger in troublesome neighborhoods. He was a mama's boy and truly cared for her. Jeanine would financially support two uncles to medical schools, my father and other uncle through engineering schools. She provided guidance and assistance to enter the U.S. and the do's and don'ts of life in America. Most importantly, Jeanine provided a home in a world unknown to her family. Jeanine would find time to not only work, support, but cook and clean. She was a lovely wife and mother.

Chapter 3: Miss You Grandma

My grandma raised me during my childhood as my parents were working to achieve a better life in Elmont, New York. Jeanine and Reynold lived with us in what would be a better home than East New York. Hard work pays off. My ancestry has taught me that no matter your circumstance as you progress in life, do not leave the past generation behind. They play a great role on how you get to where you belong. My grandma would care for me and love me. She was always around to make life better. In the later park of her life, she was wise and sharp. Remembering every descendants' birthday. Sending money and affection along with kind words. Every family member reported back to her whether for silly gossip or everyone's whereabouts and health. She was a leader that guided my family through hardships and good times. I remember her vibrant and healthy in my mind. Grandma, Jeanine, you will be missed.

Profiles in Stoicism
By
Earvin P Eugene

Chapter 1: Imperturbable

Thoughts come to me in waves like an ocean. The vastness of emotions can be overwhelming. But one must choose to be calm to weather the storm. No longer seeking approval from seniors, affection from admirers, courage from liquid. It is the time to be stoic to be left alone like on an island. Who is to know what is right or wrong? All we can do is drift ahead. It seems that a strong character is a person with grit. Someone who has endured pain and triumphs. Where do I stand? I know the grass is always greener on the other side. You would not want to trade your life for the next person unless you truly walked a day in their shoes. There is no escape from suffering. What the rich man lacks in financial troubles, the poor man gains ignorance. Ignorance is bliss. That is the course why some attempt to stay unknowledgeable. You ask why do I come here? To a young adult, not better or worse than me. I offer ventilation. A peace of mind.

Chapter 2: Why?

Stoicism by its definition is "the endurance of pain or hardship without the display of feelings and without complaint." That is a lesson we could all learn. I am trying to no longer burden others with my misfortune. This is not a profile in self-pity rather guidance to manage the disarray of life. I wish I had someone to assist me in turbulent times.

First, I had to learn to not take life too seriously. Each day is a blessing that brings forth challenges. Take the time to only perform essential activities. Remove the frivolous actions and limit leisure. Enjoy the community of family and friends but only to the extent of achieving a specific goal. There will be time for relaxation on special occasions i.e. holidays. Remove the mindset of stagnation. Improve each day, knowing you accomplished tasks. Make notes on what you need to complete the night before to complete the next day. Do not overwhelm yourself. Limit essential tasks to the most of six tasks. There will be time to splurge and release knowing you achieved success.

Second, this sounds horrible but limit travel. Retreats should not be used an escape from daily living rather an experience to gain insight into a different lifestyle one is not accustomed to. A life of travel with no learning is not beneficial. A lot of information on culture and geography can be sought out through books, videos, photos, and unique searches. Save money from travels and invest in yourself. Life should not be so intolerable that you seek constant removal from it. Make your life satisfactory to you while being ambitious. If one must travel, find your roots, and express gratitude from where you come from. Domestic travel is the best. We are all citizens of different nations. See what your country has to offer. Understand the history of your country and see where it stands today. Why are the people of your country struggling? What is your country known for? This will help you figure out where you stand in the mix of it all.

Third, do not be swayed by emotion. Be logical and concise. It is my interpretation that one must be patient yet make their own luck. Luck is the combination of preparation and opportunity. Continue to mold your life as you see fit, knowing that you are on the righteous pursuit of happiness. Life is unpredictable. The plans we make today may change tomorrow, but we can attempt to make a path for ourselves. When met with adversity find your purpose and go to it. That may be the most difficult thing. To find a passion that brings profit. Explore at a young age all your interests and see what shows promise. However, it is never too late to find purpose, but it does become more challenging to start from scratch with the responsibilities of maturity. Endure the hardship and never give up.

Next, seek refuge in labor. My mind overthinks. Therefore, I must compile my thoughts and write my ideas. To leave it on the brain with no transfer to paper, makes me exude emotion. That is not proper on the guidance to stoicism. To better myself I have been journaling for quite some time. Keeping tabs on myself by writing, expressing sadness and happiness in notes. Avoid confrontation when possible, it only leads to unsolicited stress. Leave your troubles behind. Instead form discussions with the ones you love. Converse on controversial topics and daily news. Be informed about the world around you to form your own opinions. Think freely and listen to the thoughts of people you trust and respect. Accept differences in ideology but learn something. No need for existentialism rather productivity. Be better than you were yesterday. One day you will improve on your flaws. My issues stem in disorganization. By writing this, I realize my shortcomings in certain good habits. I do not make my bed in many cases and I do not exercise as much as I should. Now, I diet and attempt to keep myself kept. By all means that's an improvement.

Chapter 3: Contentment

Lose the oppressive feeling of resentment. We live and make mistakes. Your circumstance does not define you. Keep intact close friends and family that provide comfort and compassion. Remove fake friends that led you on the wrong path. Make new connections with people that can help you. Do not be selfish. Life is give and take. Someone will provide you with something you need, and you give them something they want. It is a barter system. Appreciate the situations when you are gifted with something valuable with no cost. It is rare but all the more meaningful. God will grant you success if you match with the correct person at the right time. Remember, people come and go but the presence of a virtuous person is immeasurable. Rely on yourself on serious matters. Nobody will do the proper work for you. However, you can get by with the support from others. Nobody gets far on their own.

Contentment offers promise in the future. Trust in the process. Trust in God. With someone with trust issues, I have to succumb to a higher power and not solely on people. Be content to be alone in your thoughts. Try not to worry. Have faith in yourself. Gather all your works and present it to the right people. You will notice that someone is experiencing something similar. Life is grand yet common. My friend, who I will not mention, married at a relatively young age asked me what I want in a girl? I said pretty, knowledgeable, and relaxed in temperament and he said you need an assistant. I laughed and found it amusing but there is truth to that statement. I seek companionship in things I lack. An assistant would ameliorate the standards of my life. There is no doubt my organizational skills are faulty. Perhaps, I will be graced with the right partner in the future.

Chapter 4: Reliance

Some of us have self-medicated before. To alleviate the pain of trauma, to escape a horrible life, and for fun from dull situations. No matter the case; limit pleasure for celebrations. Pleasure is not happiness. Drugs and sex are tempting and can seem necessary in many cases but provide yourself limitations. Accept your vice and forfeit to satisfaction only after accomplishments. This is the first step for me. Maybe a night cap or relaxation with friends or family on the weekends and holidays. There must be management of wicked behavior. Knowing myself I could not live a completely dry life at the moment. Expectations battle reality time and again.

Do as the doctor says for a long life. Only if you could eat an apple a day to keep him away. Face your health and make a choice for longevity or quick excitement. Healthcare professionals play a strong role in managing medication and therapy, but the job is not theirs alone. You must decide how to self-medicate and gain treatment.

Chapter 5: Acceptance

What have we learned? To be true to oneself. Expect the unexpected. Adjust my life accordingly. To remain calm when tides of sorrow reach your shore. Be steadfast, embracing the ups and downs of good and bad fortune. Look inward to tackle your trials and tribulations and push outward with dedication in a craft. Accept the fact that nobody is perfect. Accept the life we are given and that in work, we will find salvation. Accept the good, the bad, and the ugly.

Wasted Ramifications
Subtitle: I Just Wanted You To Know
By
Earvin Eugene

Chapter 1: Drinks On Us

All he wanted was a seat at the table. Christian worked ambitiously in engineering.

Grueling hours on constant projects. From six in the morning to three in the afternoon Monday through Friday. Sometimes overtime if he needed the money. Work kept him busy and he was glad he could support himself. However, he felt empty.

Chris came from a poor neighborhood in New York. So, to go to college and make something of himself was more than expected of him. In America it seems that the safe way is the best way to get ahead. Go to school and work like a dog to make it out of poverty. Is this the American Dream? It was once said "Education is the passport to the future, for tomorrow belongs to those who prepare for it today." At the present, times have become harder. One must be literate and take risks. No risk no reward.

Christian was a serious guy, who unraveled with a few drinks to an outgoing fellow.

That was his vice. After a long days work, he unwind with a drink or two. He would consider starting a family, but he was unaware of the responsibilities. Could he be a good father? Chris is twenty-eight years old now. In this generation it is more and more difficult to live the traditional lifestyle of our forefathers. He could understand Make America Great Again not for politics but for the resolve in a picturesque United States. A location where with a plan and commitment, you could live a sustainable life. A house with your own freedoms, a family, cars, and a stable job.

Now, with greed, one must fend for themself. The ladder to success has no clear path.

You want to go up but do not know how. Continuing the guidance from our seniors appear to be suitable but it is out of touch with the demands of today. Wisdom cannot be overlooked so, perhaps it's best to take the good from the past and develop some new strategy for the future. Who has the answers?

Chris noticed bounty in successful people. If he can make it so can I. The life of lavish, respect, and power. He was not ignorant to the fact that they were determined but they must possess some sort of connection or real advice. He wanted a piece of the pie.

Therefore, he paid for friendship. It was the cost of opportunity. He had plans to meet with the rich individuals, Pete and Jacob. He went to the business partners and from their website made a transaction to meet. They owned a publishing Agency.

Phoenix Publishing LLC. They developed online products from eBooks to website applications. They were quite notable and only interacted with socialites. The two attended exclusive gatherings and for a limited time allowed new guests to meet through payments. Most expected it to be a paid meet and greet. Or some life changing support. But, Chris new all too well it was an occasion to mix business with pleasure for them.

At first there was little small talk exchanged between Christian and the two elite.

It would be quick conversations of facts. They all understood that time is money.

After some time, the two leaders gained a liking to Chris as they saw promise in him.

They knew it would be lucrative to meet with him. It did not hurt that Chris was likeable and funny. See, he wanted to be a published writer. Chris had a lot of ideas to share on the world. His feedback was valuable. The two enjoyed his thoughts, style, and demeanor.

Chris wanted a seal of trust from the insiders to stamp his place in the world.

The three agreed to meet at an expensive bar in New York City. The two ended the last email with "Drinks are on us".

Chapter 2: Wasted

It was a serene night. In the city that doesn't sleep, it was bright in the dark. It was beautiful and silent bar. Christian could never be accepted without the help of his partners.

It was a brand-new world. Pete ordered rounds of jack and coke. You could tell they were self-made. Jacob said "What is your book? Why should we publish you?"

Chris finished his drink and stated, "It's called Heartless". It was about a struggling writer who found promise with the help of friends, family, and his supporters. The writer had problems with mental health and drug addiction. He lost everything but found redemption with luck. He stole works and past them on as his own until he committed to a magnificent manuscript in drug fueled passion. Against all odds, he created a masterpiece. The two were satisfied. Pete stated, "send me more of your works". Jacob told Chris let's talk privately. Chris bought himself a gin and tonic. Jacob ordered a diamond cocktail and mentioned "You should of bought us drinks". Christian said, "Next time". Jacob said.

"We're interested but we need some more." Chris would normally be frustrated but the drinks calmed his nerves.

Pete and Jacob went to order more drinks and privately discussed marketing, finances, and women. Christian was alone with his thoughts. He would have anxiety from the uncertainty but the drinks relaxed him. Pete put his arm around Chris and told him, "You're going to be rich one day." Christian thought what do I know, he didn't have the best judgement at the moment. Pete and Jacob seemed well equipped under these conditions. Pete said, "What do you want?" Chris happily stated "Success!" Pete had an idea, you send us more manuscripts and set specific guidelines for the project and we will establish a deal. Christian thinking this is how the industry works, hesitantly stated "Sure". Pete brought Chris back to the table with Jacob waiting. It was only the three of them, but he felt the world on his shoulders.

Chapter 3: Ramifications

The three of them enjoyed one more round of drinks. Christian felt he was on his path to success. Jacob and Peter were ecstatic, but their appearance seemed sinister. The two said you know we make our published books international and available to all the best retailers. Christian knew this as a fact and simply nodded. They all shook hands as good practice. Girlfriends of Jacob and Pete arrived. Two beautiful girls Christian never seen before. You could tell that they were young and loved to party. No more business was discussed. It was only pleasure now. The night would go on all night.

HYPE
By
Earvin Eugene

Chapter 1: Key

On an island there was mystic beauty. Majestic with beaches, palm trees, and clear skies. Who knew a legend would start here. Michael Brown was a man of the world. He was staying at shared home with other Americans and international individuals. They all came here with the same purpose of studying.

It was part of this grant that advocated students to travel abroad to learn about new cultures. The material was complicated and conflicted with the relaxed atmosphere of Caribbean life. Moreover, classmates would learn during the day and adventure at night. The students amusingly considered the residence as a "safe house". A two story home with multiple apartments at the corner of the tropical city. The school was magnificent. Many stories with transparent glasses. You could feel the warmth from the island.

Advanced technology made the institution sophisticated with teachers from many different countries.

The main spoken language was English. You could tell the professors were well educated and versed about different cultures. On the surface, they were ideal role models. The school was the most extravagant object in the town in modern terms. The city had strong traditions of spicy homegrown food, fishing, swimming, festivals, and simple trading amongst citizens. You could view the edges of the island surrounded by mountains protecting the people from the harsh pretty ocean. The inhabitants were dark-skinned but did posses a select amount of mixed-beauties. The entire population had exotic attractive islanders.

Shops were small. The most lucrative places which were few were from outsourced powers. The majority of people traded by hand, the best objects were collected by word of mouth.

The major players at the "safe house" were Sakina, Alyssa, and Faiz. Each possessed their own living quarters at the house. Sakina was a friend of Michael's sister, she was accepted due to her connections with legacy students. Alyssa was a superficial girl who enjoyed to party, she attended the program due to her family's money. Faiz was a Pakistani guy, who spent some time in the United States studying and transferred to this prestigious program due to good grades. In addition, Michael just made it to the program due to good fortune and luck. He was an average student, came from a middle-class family, and knew few people prior to entering the school except Sakina. Michael was fun, caring, and quite interesting.

Maybe he won the interviewers over with his great personality and charisma.

Chapter 2: Secrets

Sakina was black and white. Possessing the best of two worlds. She was tall and had long braided hair.

Bright brown eyes and full lips. Her skin tone was a tan yellow. She enjoyed the rigorous studies and excelled. However, she was irresponsible and found ways to achieve success without ambitious work.

She usually got by accessing information from other classmates. This did not only apply to school, she used people to get ahead in many aspects of life. Michael would spend time with Sakina on several occasions even though he knew she was using him for resources. Michael spoke on the phone with his sister, Natalie, "How's life?" and other small talk. Natalie said, "Do not hangout with Sakina, she is a bad influence."

Natalie loved Michael and knew he was easily influenced by others. Natalie helped Sakina get in the program for good karma but was not true friends with Sakina. It was only a friendship on the surface. Michael was very aware of the situation. He replied to Natalie, "I love you, I'll be a good boy". They were satisfied with their conversation, knowing both said their part. Michael and Natalie would check on each other throughout Michael's time in the program. One day, Sakina asked Michael for some answers for a particular homework. He went to her bedroom. Michael grew up in strict household and did not drink much. Sakina was an advent drinker. She had numerous bottles of vodka and some sort of mixed alcoholic lemonade flavored drink. Sakina drank from the vodka while Michael drank from the homemade cocktail. He gave her the answers to the homework but wanted something in return. They kissed and had sex in what would be drunk passion. When finished, Michael stated "Do not tell my sister". Now more sober, Sakina was slightly upset but agreed. It seemed there was a possibility that Sakina wanted to be a part of Michael's family. But they were not a suitable match. They would mutually go their separate ways.

It was a secret memory.

Faiz was responsible. He had to work very hard to get in the position he was in. He was a devout Muslim.

This prevented him from partaking in the many pastimes of traditional American culture. He fasted at times and strayed away from pre-marital sex, drugs, alcohol. His most dangerous vice was sneaking a cigarette at the end of a laborious day of studying. Michael enjoyed Faiz Pakistani tea in the morning before school.

It was similar to the British culture of tea. Pakistan has a lot of British influence historically. They would vent to each other about the everyday struggles of life. Even though they had a very different upbringing, every man has the same urge for sex and are confused on how to reach their goals. They would exercise together and motivate each other to be productive. Michael with his new freedom away from parents would dabble in bad behavior. He would tell Faiz to hold his liquor to prevent himself from abusing alcohol. He would occasional take gulps after a stressful exam. Faiz would monitor him while smoking his cigarettes.

On a specific night, Michael and Faiz ordered a lady of the night from a local. Michael gained confidence from the booze as he never did this before. Faiz sober and horny broke one of his religious rules. They both had sex with her. Faiz paid for both of them. Michael said "I'll pay you back".

Alyssa found comfort in drugs. She was addicted to cocaine. When she could not have the right amount she would smoke weed and drink. She was pretty but not well equipped for school. Alyssa just saw the program as a pit spot to party and vacation on an island. She had a boyfriend each one fulfilling a different purpose it seems. One, tall to reach things around the house and be fitted to perform physical activities.

Another, for money when her dad would not send her any and several others. One time, Michael and Alyssa agreed to meet at Michael's place to study. She was on the phone with her father. The conversation ended.

Michael interested said "What were you talking about?" Alyssa replied "My dad is on Hydrochlorothiazide"

Michael wanted to impress her by telling her a scientific fact that Hydrochlorothiazide was for blood pressure.

She surprisingly said "I do not give a fuck." He was shocked. They studied for a short time but Alyssa was impatient and bored. She asked Michael for money. He gave her the small spare cash he had. She thanked him with a kiss and left. The next time, Michael drove Alyssa around in his car. It was rare for a student on the island to use their own car. Alyssa found use in Michael. To Michael's dismay, she brought a male companion. The three drove around the island finding serene locations to take in while smoking cigarettes. She left with the guy privately to talk. Alyssa high on drugs was unaware she was kissing her friend noticeably by Michael. He thought this girl is trouble. As they drove back, Michael brought to the attention of Alyssa his disappointment in her. She would not acknowledge his disapproval. She was disrespectful but kissed Michael. Back at the "safe house", the two drank some alcohol and had sex. Alyssa was bad at sex. She was pretty but emotionless. She felt that Michael should be grateful to just be in her presence. After communicating for a few more weeks, the two would eventually stop.

Chapter 3: Finale

Michael now failing in the program, thought it was time to salvage whatever money he had left and pursue a new path. He spoke to his family to make arrangements to go home. He gained a lot of experience on the cay but was too young to give it one hundred percent. Michael needed to learn more about life before expecting to receive this responsibility. Many of his colleagues failed as well. He enjoyed the last night on the balcony of the "safe house" staring at the full moon. He thought of a brand-new tomorrow.

The moonlight lit up the whole island. It was a sight to see.

Redemption
Subtitle: Who Is Going To Save Me From Myself?
By
Earvin Eugene

Chapter 1: Experiences

A guy meets a young girl. He is introduced to her through a friend. They like him, because he has a car and they do not. Little did they know he would want something in return. It was a double date across the town. All four picked up food at the drive thru and parked themselves at the park at night.

They spit the shit and ate the food. Young, they were glad to just be away from their parents' supervision. Out in the world, in what seemed like freedom. One of the guys of the group starts kissing and making advances with his date in the backseat of the car. The protagonist states, "What are they doing?" His date laughs and says "I do not know". He took this as an opportunity to start making moves on his date. They kissed and he was able to touch her wherever he pleased.

He thought this was worth the drive. On another occasion, he spent time with his real friends. They were driving now and he was in the backseat with the same girl. After their first experience together, he thought it was acceptable to make moves on the girl whenever he pleased.

Therefore, he kissed the girl and felt her up. She was not pleased. She returned the favor but said, "I do not want to do this right now". He was upset but settled down. All his friends rejoiced at the fact that he kissed her. They did not believe that he hooked up with her in the past. They drove around aimlessly, hoping he could seal the deal. With no luck they just had fun talking and driving.

On what would be expecting to be a great day, the guy made plans to host a party at his house.

His parents were skeptical to allow him to party but they thought better at home than making trouble elsewhere. In this situation, many friends arrived and his older brother could join along.

Providing the alcohol to the festivities. The older brother made advances at the younger brother's girl.

The girl being promiscuous played innocent. The guy was angry and fueled with alcohol. He was usually playful when drunk but this time was different. He confronted his brother in front of everyone and said "fuck you". The two brothers had exchanges and the guy made a scene. His parents were upset and thought he was an angry drunk. The party would settle back into groove after the guy had a talk with his family. The promiscuous girl flirted with several guys at the party with no advances. As she understood this was not the time and place to sell herself at the guy's house. However, it was in her nature to attract male attention. All in all, the party would be a success. As the guy got a few girls' numbers. And he knew a new girlfriend could be a possibility.

The two brothers settled their disputes.

The guy learned a lesson that these girls are for everybody and loss his belief in monogamy.

A few weeks later, his closest friend was driving with him. The guy invited the younger girls including the promiscuous girl. He thought he could let bygones be bygones and still be in her presence. She did not belong to him but she could possibly hook up with him from time to time. The guy's closest friend did not respect these girls and wanted no business with them. The girls wanted to stop at the store and buy alcohol. So, the guy's friend drove to the location and the two waited in the car as the girls went to buy the booze. As the girls were inside the guy's friend said "I do not want anything to do with these girls". The guy not feeling consideration for his friend or the girls, simply said "Okay?". His friend said "I'm leaving". The guy wanted the company of the girl but his friend was the one driving the car so he had no real choice in the matter. The guy's friend drove the car and left the girls behind.

The girls were stranded with no ride and the guy's friend laughed. Perhaps, the guy did wrong by condoning his friend and leaving the girls stranded but he did have some disdain for the promiscuous girl. The two friends would play video games and drink instead. They had a strong bond at the time. The guy's friend said "Who needs those girls." The guy just wanted an escape from the burden of typical life and spent his time drinking and spending time with his friend.

Chapter 2: Two of a kind

A boy and his best friend were set to spend time together. Due to struggling times, both were still living with their parents. They both struggled with mental health issues and were pessimistic of the world. The boy went to his friend's house to watch sports. Due to his recent hospitalization, his sister had to drop him off at his friend's house. The boy's parents did not trust him with the car. When he arrived his friend greeted him with open arms. They were glad to see each other. The friend said, "It's been long overdue". He agreed. They smoked a cigarette and conversed on past parties, high school moments together, and how they were handling their troubles. The conversation was not too serious. Once they finished, the boy was welcomed inside the house. The friend's parents were glad to see him. They discussed plans for the future and exchanged small talk. The boy went to his father's special room with World War Two memorabilia. The boy educated in history had a compelling discussion with the friend's father about D-day. The father had a complete miniature re-enactment of the battle. They joked it was lucky that the Allied forces won or they would not be here.

The boy went to the basement with his friend. They drank beers at watched the islanders hockey game on the television. They forgot their troubles and enjoyed the game. The friend said, "Are you talking to any girls at the moment?" The boy said "No". His friend stated, "Me neither". At their peak, the two would party with all the pretty girls in town. They wished to be with them right now.

In order to spice things up they took Ativan. Which is Ill-advised when drinking. But life is short.

They talked about the medications they were taking. His friend said how he needed Ativan and how he was not the same without it. The boy had his stint with the drug but was all too aware of its addictive properties. He only took it from time to time now. The two were quite high now. They laughed and enjoyed the game. They talked about other friends and recapped on how they were doing. It seemed everyone was struggling but they did not get caught up in negativity.

It was time for the boy to leave. As a parting gift, the friend gave him an Ativan for the road. He walked him to the porch and smoked one last cigarette until his sister would arrive to pick them up. The boy realized everyone was fighting a demon inside. He left and the two did not speak much in the future. They were getting older and it was time to find a path forward. The older you get, it seems the less close friends spend time together. You have to get married and find a job. Support your family and gain independence from your parents. The two had a long way to go.

Chapter 3: Celebration

It was the boy's birthday. He did not enjoy the celebration of the day but those around him who cared would apply all the festivities. The day started normally with breakfast. His mother made his favorite; scrambled eggs with cheese and maple sausage. His mother loved him. She wanted the best for him. She wanted him to appreciate his birthday. Another year older, another year wiser.

Next, he made plans to go to the local mall for a date. The girl knew it was his birthday and wanted to show him affection. They met at the Starbucks in the mall. The boy and the girl drank their coffee and the girl paid knowing it was his birthday. They walked around enjoying the stores. It was leisure.

They talked about their favorite things. The boy liked money, sports, and hip hop music. The girl enjoyed traveling, food, and fashion. The boy received notice that his parents wanted to eat out at his favorite Chinese buffet restaurant. He told the girl, he had to go. She kissed him goodbye. They walked outside to his car. She liked his white Jeep. She said that car is not like you. She went back inside the mall and he drove to meet his parents at the restaurant.

At the Chinese buffet his parents greeted him. They were assigned a nice table. They ordered drinks and water. His dad gave him a birthday card with sentimental words from the family. To paraphrase, it said something like "May God grant you peace, wealth, and happiness". Enclosed was twenty dollars. That could be useful in the future. The boy liked to save and collect things, including money. They enjoyed the limitless food until they were full. His parents mentioned "You are growing up to be a handsome young man". The boy did not take compliments well and simply replied, "Thank you". During the family time he was texted the girl he hanged out with earlier.

She wanted him to go to back to the mall. She messaged "I have a surprise for you". The boy told his parents that he wanted to go back to the mall to spend time with the girl. His parents were glad that he was enjoying his birthday and told him "We'll see you at home". The boy left and went to the mall.

It was night now. The boy and girl met at the mall again. The girl was ecstatic. She told him, "Let us go to your car". The two in the dark started to kiss. The boy touched all over soft skin.

He pulled the seat back and the girl went down on him for what seemed like a lifetime. The boy enjoyed every second of it. The girl wanted to take things a step further. However, the boy did not have a condom. There was nothing he could do. The two played around and kissed for a few more moments. She said "Happy Birthday". The girl said I have a ride home. They parted ways.

She vanished into the night. The boy thought to himself, "This was not a bad birthday".

Chapter 4: Social Gathering

A guy was to attend several fraternity parties. It was pledging season. At one frat party, he went with his friends for morale support. They walked to the fraternity house together. They laughed and made jokes on their way. It was a break from all the stresses of the world. At arrival, everyone was having a blast. The hosts were glad they came. The guy played beer pong with his friend as his partner. They would win some games and lose others. He was too drunk to be completely competitive. He vaped his nicotine as he walked around the party conversing with friends. He was in good company. What caught his eye was a short brunette girl with bright eyes. She was a party monster. She was sociable and fun. She danced on the table. She was a great sensual dancer.

It reminded him of a naive stripper. He wanted to her his. If only she could be tamed. He spoke to her for a little bit. She flirted and he returned the favor. He was wise enough to know that this was her nature. She loves everybody. She was just being friendly. Nonetheless there was a spark of attraction but nothing could be done.

The guy would continue to have more drinks. More than he was accustomed to. He sat down for a moment. He stared with a blank expression on his face at the people of the party. Girls and other guys would come to check on him. He was okay. He just enjoyed the booze too much.

He wanted to soak it all in. The friends asked him "Do you like the fraternity?" He told them "I do".

Chapter 5: Gambling

A young man and his friend decided to the casino. He never been before. He thought why not see what it is all about. The bright lights were enticing. The smell of tobacco and money were intriguing. The sight of pretty girls dancing on stage rhythmically. The sound of exciting music was amazing. This was the place to be. The friend showed him the ropes. How to make a bet, who to talk to about what, and the best ways to enjoy yourself. The guy was simply glad at the fact that there was a place where you could smoke, drink, and make money.

The guy was too frugal to truly bet big money. Especially since this was his first time in new territory.

He played the slot machines, games, and places meager bets on basketball. So far he walked away with winning five dollars.

Chapter 6: High Off Life

There was a boy who always acted mischievously anytime his parents were away. On one hot Summer day as both his parents were gone at work he met one of his friends. They usually in a sneaky fashion smoked marijuana and cigarettes. They were out of resources and money. They knew their parents would not send them money at this time. They were overprotective and overbearing. They would question as to why they need the money and would escalate to drama.

It was a shame they were addicted at such a young age. They fiend the supplies.

The boy went to his local convenient store. He did not know what came over him. There was a long line at the store. He went behind the counter and took a pack of cigarettes. He went to the counter with what spare money he had and offered to pay the owner. The worker ignored him.

The boy was upset. He put the money down on the counter and started walking out of the store.

The worker said I'm calling the police. Not knowing what to do, the boy left the money on the counter and left with the pack of smokes.

While driving with his friend, smoking cigarettes, he received an alarming call from his phone.

His parents were terrified and disturbed. They screamed over the phone "Come home!". When he arrived it was havoc. His parents brought to his attention that the police arrived asking of his whereabouts. They were fueled with anger. He learned his lesson to have patience.

www.ingramcontent.com/pod-product-compliance
Lightning Source LLC
Chambersburg PA
CBHW080922160726
48000CB00009B/3094